Disturbed Sleep

M. Kaat Toy

FUTURECYCLE PRESS
www.futurecycle.org

Published by FutureCycle Press
Hayesville, North Carolina, USA

ISBN 978-1-938853-17-3

Contents

Outlands

Waterways

Musings

Decompositions

Sightings

Outbreaks

*For all the angelic spirits
and galactic beings assisting us.*

"We are late, but we are not too late."

*—from the International Council of Thirteen
Indigenous Grandmothers*

Outlands

At the Summer Refectory

*Baked slowly under sun-slathered glass, green apples sliced
thin against endless hunger release their sequestered sweetness.
All our dissatisfaction is just ancient tapestry we need to stop
holding our heraldry up to.*

Burying the Dead Horse

He shoes the horse for six years. Always a struggle, the thing
bites him on the ass as he hammers; sinks its mean, yellow teeth
into his worn jeans; kicks with its shoes half-finished, sand and new
metal flying. Sometimes the farrier puts a chain around the horse's
upper lip, asks the owner to pull it tight. Sometimes he blindfolds
him or ties him into his stall. For six years he saves the shoeing fee
until he has enough—$1,500—to buy the horse, lead him home,
dig him a grave, and make him lie down.

Pueblo Dog

"There's a carcass in your yard," my friend's new neighbor says one spring day while the snow is melting. My friend is too embarrassed to say it had been her dog, the family pet, a large golden retriever mix. Years before, he was born a pueblo dog, and he lived a pueblo dog's life, never once showing any interest in going indoors. Old, suffering from arthritis, when he went missing she searched for him and called the shelter. She hadn't thought of looking all the way in the back, she tells me. Together, she and her new neighbor put the bones in the trash.

Churchyard Statuary

The lichen-mottled angel came to life tonight. He was kneeling,
hands in a pyramid before his chest, in front of the statue of Mary;
then, he stood up. His eyes shimmered, shifting between this
world and the next, or between being a believer and one who
cannot believe, one of the forgiven or one of the unwashed.
Or maybe it was just the medication surging like a current that
made his eyes go bright then dim when I asked if he was doing
all right. He was doing all right, he said, and though I was sure
he wasn't lying, I was sorry for all the damage the lichen had done.

Momentary Disorganization

Striving to sustain full speed as crossing headlights split the stillness I had sought before sunrise, I watched my confused feet leave the sidewalk, my arms level in the air, the sandy pavement pass beneath me. I felt sad for myself. I pulled my palms up, decided not to scar my knees again. I was willing to land anywhere else. But when you hit chin first, you find out how hard the world is. It makes you spit out your teeth, hold closed the hole where your skin no longer is, and run not so fearlessly, so out of control.

Dolor

A little girl in pink, her daddy's buttoned shirt matching, in portrait studio pictures exploding larger than love from the office walls of the most unhappy man alive, the poet who dedicated his book "To Sabina, positively" before their divorce dumped him two thousand miles away. When I greet him, he grows darker and more suspicious until his cell phone—his preferred companion—redirects him. I walk away trying to dissipate the spreading burden this sensei has become. Some people don't know where their essential parts are, their emotions are so governed by strict laws.

Obedience School

"I just got out of surgery," he says, raising his pale, drugged face from the classroom table as I, a synthesized instructor at this obedience school, walk in. "AND I'M HIS MOTHER," announces a blonde woman ten years younger than I am. Snowboarding, he broke his collarbone just below the metal plate left from another snowboarding accident. The doctor said it was good his arm was already in a cast protecting his wrist, broken skateboarding, from being broken again.

Before becoming this apparition, he had e-mailed me, twice, asking if this, his fourth absence, could be excused. I referred him, twice, to the attendance policy which says "No excused absences FOR ANY REASON." Students e-mail and ask me about my attendance policy relentlessly, sometimes as many as five a day.

My ersatz student starts to go. "I'm not going to mark you here then have you leave," I tell him, watching for his mother to seize me or have a spurious seizure. They negotiate arrangements; then, she departs. He puts his head down and sleeps. Another student says, "He shouldn't be here," as if it were my fault for making him attend.

After class, my representative of three-D reality apologizes, but the only thing that helps is knowing someday, if we learn our lessons, our DNA will shift—our bodies will become crystalline—conscious light and sound—they won't get damaged—we won't get sick—we can even be in two places at once—and one of them won't have to be work.

The Trail of Prayers to Gaia's Twins

At fourteen, Gaia, praying at her friend's church, went deep into her heart to get them: Her mother's boyfriend had molested her, so she testified against him and her mother who had sheltered him; now they were in jail. It was her same-age foster sister who was with her during the ultrasound when the nurse said, "Here is your baby," then, moving the instrument, added, surprising everyone, "and here is your *other* baby." Gaia was thrilled. She had always wanted boy and girl twins, if you could call fourteen years "always."

Now her trials began. They would need more than she could provide, she discovered doing the homework assigned by the foster care system. Her foster mother, who hoarded the state money to feed the foster children she raised, wanted them; so holding fast to her swelling belly, Gaia prayed until other couples came. But through their father, the twins were Native American; only a Native American family could have them, Gaia learned. One couple who prayed with her often recalled their grandmother had tribal enrollment papers, though no one could find them. When they all prayed more, the papers appeared.

Here in rural Oklahoma where the Trail of Tears led, this is the story the twins will learn when they are old enough to understand; but now, while Gaia is eighteen, what the couple tells them is that they came from Gaia's belly—"Gaia" is what they all call her when she is with them during college vacations—and what the twins know is that they love Gaia, the earthly mother who carried them; and in my office, when Gaia tells me she loves telling her story, I am the one crying because Gaia never doubted the power of her prayers.

Undernourished and Overfed

In penance for the pleasure of consuming others' food alone,
on the longest, darkest night of the year I prepare porridge for
three unwell, uncaring bachelor bears, uncertain if these creatures
reflect my flaws or are apparitions I can walk away from. First, Big
Bear, six foot four and three hundred pounds, staggers in bracing
his overburdened back. "Open the goddamn window! My room is
too goddamn hot!" he yells, shoving the slider back. "I'm sorry,"
I softly say. Thinking of how clean and quiet I was being, I spaced
the temperature out. "Bullshit!" he bellows with an angry twist to
his huge, arrogantly held head. "I'm sorry," I peacefully insist as
he stomps off. Next, Baby Bear, short and fat from foraging on
thrown-out food, enters crying "This is emotional blackmail!" and
waving the self-promotion letter I, his imaginary *amore,* corrected
for him. The "we" who paid to plant a community garden on his
vacant land wasn't the same "we" who sponsored his anti-poverty
tour through Mexico, I pointed out. "But it's all true!" he protests.
"I did go to Mexico. I did work on the garden. I can't remember
the names and details." "You aren't a nonprofit charity," I counter.
"You're just one person doing what you please." He huffs then
returns to the plush baby bears he conducts to the symphony of
praise echoing in his head, his way of nursing his PTSD brought on
by frequent trips to jail. Finally, grey-haired, bearded Middle Bear
toddles in barefoot, stomach protruding, bringing a plastic bag
of wild birds' eggs, blueberries, roots, and leaves, more strange
remedies for his Lyme disease. This self-confessed misanthropist
opens the refrigerator and, hauling my lettuce and spinach out,
shouts, "Why don't you fix this for all of us? You're taking too
much space! Next time you bring home groceries, I'll lock you out!"
I respond, "You're not very nice. You take more space than anyone.
You have stuff on every shelf." He retorts, "You're not the most
amusing friend. Why don't you move?" Surprised he can conceive
of an amusing friend, I reply, "I will, as soon as I can." After all,
it is my house we are living in.

Waterways

In an Off-Season Sublet Where Beeswax and Ambergris Burn

Naked, cross-legged, we melt against the ocean-gray floor.
The sea wind tempers us. Buddha looks on. We are breathing out,
and we are breathing in.

Far Harbor

The sky is not the transcendent subject though its spread is awe-striking: The clouds are like waves, and the waves are like waves—shifting dull silver. The clouds and the waves are like mirrors—old, expansive, silver mirrors—cracked into waves, misted into clouds—like the mirror I see myself transformed in as I watch silver dissolving. The transcendent subject is what's between the cracks and the silver, the mist and the sky, the clouds and the mirror; what it takes to get there; what it takes to get away.

Gallery Talk

"The heads are useless," the painter explains. "They don't
work anymore. So I gather around me friends from the natural
world—flowers relieved of their vibrancy; seedpods dried and
broken open; bones of animals from air, water, and land. They bring
me the news—releasing me from personal history like the flood that
washed through my studio. A shriving. Every day I put the news
down in shrines that celebrate not making but that which is
already made—made for us. They emanate energy. Great beings
of light here to help us remember what we are and who we are
show themselves—the interface between the possible and
the impossible."

Desert Passages

In a way, it's crazy. It's backwards. The form of something very functional becomes the theater of what we are doing. The earth is shaped by wind and water. The shadows express the structure of the view. The photos document the process of time with no control over the framing, lighting, or decisive moment. Seep, spring, creek, arroyo, wash: What came out here is put over there. If you set sheets of glass in the soil at angles, the water will find a way around them. If you set them in a square, they'll collapse. The essence of landscape is culture and nature stepping on each other's shoulders wanting to change something.

Our River Guardians

They're dying now, especially the small, quiet ones. Sad faces
hidden beneath blue clay, they pine for the cloud springs they
came from. Already few remained, escaped to the serrated, snowy
mountains to protect the knowledge given to them. Mirroring their
ancestral sky burials, their hidden platforms on high stilts surround
us as they peer through their viewports at all the devil, God's elder
brother, the more powerful one, created. We pray for them to pray
for us, to keep the link unbroken with the bountiful world above
that feeds us as we lie, face up, mouths gaping, in the cold, swift
stream, doing our thing, not noticing all they are doing for us, not
knowing why they came here or why they draw symbols in another
language upon the air.

The Bardo of Our Idolatry

What would we know if we didn't know anything? More than we do now. Reincarnation was never meant to happen; life was meant to be a circular flow from Creator to Creation, not canal locks of repeatedly learning we are one entity, one identity, embodying all twelve dimensions in the same time and space. The opportunity for liberation draws us to this transitional state where consciousness is not connected to the physical body. Here we choose the cataracts we'll disappear into in each intelligent, responsive world. As one spiritual field submerges and another turbulent confluence rushes up, with abandon we cultivate our inability to be out of control and find something we didn't intend to find, where we won't really go anywhere, but we'll have a really good time.

El Gordo

The fruit stand president stamps transportation papers with
pretty food pictures for those of us returning from the bottom of
the sea where we somehow slipped from between the cracks when
our cruise ship hit a reef of deep unconsciousness during supper.
A thin man, bundled against the cold, looks on, waiting for the plain
white rice he asks for every two or three years, while I eat fast, a
vulture capitalist gorging on the delicious, hot culture I have been
raised on, in love with myself, assuming everyone else is in love
with me. The man is part of the one percent bringing into existence
we other ninety-nine riding in white chariots of future rebellion
pulled by black stallions of unmanifested power. He never wanted
to be bigger like El Gordo, the galaxy cluster. He always wanted to
go the other way.

Errata

At the polymorphous I Migrant Motel, the fearless rose virgin who can't read or write English waits for a teacher who will teach her. Babies have arrived faster, icons of contact of the numinous with the natural world, small Christs hanging crucified from window-sills, sunlight illuminating them, evidence of the ultimate presence of Being and a diffused, free offering of love. Unsuited for work, they call to their fathers fleeing barefoot through the snow while the virgin's amanuensis writes her story in neon red—a vehicle to stop a righteous orgy of indignation. *You should have disappeared years ago,* it begins, *before you transcended the bonds of materialism.* Outside citizenship, this border-crossing woman, paid to juggle other people's property, dreams of tall ships to return her to her island people who send her seashells, her most cherished possessions. No single category contains her, she defies them all, as she places sugar cookies on the tongues of the marginalized masses dancing to tribal talking drums calling in an apocalypse of just redistribution.

Super-Slip Boundary Conditions

As she watched the birds wheel overhead, time would lose its meaning for her, she being in resonance with her calling. With the whorling limbs of the fig tree she spoke in their succulent language of water. When friends took her fishing, she threw down her pole and went in after them. Eating them anointed with olive oil and rosemary, her soul burned white as Jesus's. But back at work she was thrown into a locked position—threatening and aggressive. Her computer telepathy misfired. She couldn't integrate the waves coming in. Cataclysmic planetary events became possible. At the hospital, Marian maids dressed in red with Robin Hood green pointed caps ministered to her with hands on as synaptic jolts arrived faster. Returning from a visit in hyperspace, she missed the Jupiter corridor, setting up a sonic boom. In the mountains, rivers slid up their sides, twisting over their rocky paths in a high state of polarization and turmoil. "God, make this blood go away," her husband had prayed in the past, and it did, the lurid mess from her bitten tongue completely disappearing. He didn't understand why this time she wasn't going to wake up.

Musings

Dido's Inferno

The cage of my emotions grows smaller bar by bar as I become boxed in by my hunger to be full of the fruits of love: quince, strawberry, watermelon—all red, juicy, and sweet when ripened and prepared correctly. All could be contained here, occupying the pyre now filled with longing, fire, and flames if longing, fire, and flames could fill a blackened, no-man's-land place.

The Subterraneans Submit

Above ground, the exquisite, squirming lies about separateness
and exclusivity made the whole thing die below where there had
been so much life—or so many past lives—attracting these two
in a grand, grotesque way: Erebos and Nyx, darkness and night,
spooled around each other engendering vitality. Rebels such as
them wanted to dance outside time or deep inside it where the cave
filled with their dried funeral flowers was hidden in the flagrant
mists enveloping the world's edges. Who wouldn't want to go there?
No debts to pay. Just untold tickets for their favorite ride home that
they couldn't stop taking, secretly thanking each other for it and for
something that filled them beyond bread and duties. Telephones
disconnected in their presence, not that they were together often.
Sensing society's surfeit of unsustainable stunts, they produced
steady shocks of survival warnings; but when the required artifices
sucked up more air than it took to construct them, more air than
their cells held, they separated forever and returned, soulless,
to the sunshine where sterile gods and goddesses circulate
unleashed.

Horus in Struggle

Winging through the sky Nile on sentry duty from his universe
to the Land of Craft, the all-seeing savant with the falcon head
balances the hours between his right eye, the sun, and his left, the
moon, guided by his gateway planets, Sirius and Venus. Uniting
celestial and terrestrial forces, this protector of men and animals
tracts the highway of electricity alternating between bodies. A
prophet of philosophy dreaming of a common language for his
divided territory, he, never sleeping, monitors man's desire to
dominate all nature and spread havoc. Through inscrutable
mindknots of interference generated by his subjects' overreaching,
he insures the cycles of alluvial plain flooding that Hathor, his all-
wife, brings to fruition. Concentrating keenly to align with the
distant harmonies he hears, he follows the nightingale, his only
companion in the darkness. Drunken on the beauty of this lonely
male's seductive song, the solemn overseer of traditions loses his
focus, swinging further and further from his course, until a vortex
of fragmentation sucks him into the big, black bowl of fortune
covering the world, and, with a clash and flash, the oneness
of dissolution takes him home.

Parading Without a Permit

On the world stage, Ophelia wore a lavender gauze gown in a shade pale enough to see through to let people know she wasn't all there and no longer cared to hide it. Its lightness used to weigh on her as another unforgivable trespass, but now, drifting on its wings in between to be and not to be, it is a blessing like everything: Hamlet's feigned madness, her own madness unavoidably sincere, the branch she laid herself to sleep on breaking over this shallow brook, its escape opening up.

The angry differences eroding a chasm between her and everyone she had ever known or was likely to had changed from a river of bitter rue to this sweet, floating violet repast: Bathing herself in others' pain, she experienced the wonder of their having survived it, a glut of gratitude filling the span inside her where, judging others lacking, a strait had opened up.

"I stopped you because I was wondering if you were all right," the policeman said, growing larger the longer she stared up at him. "Did I mess up somewhere?" she asked, touching the wound on her forehead and examining the blood. Nodding, he answered, "At least we know you're alive." Searching for some truth in this, she enumerated to herself all the arrests that had impeded her character development. "Parts of me anyway," she replied.

Relinquishing Underwater Parallax Delirium

Our shell-shocked hero patiently observed the worst mountebank roofers led by a Cyclops remove the shingles on his rented, two-bedroom duplex, the one his wife, a dislocated military brat like they both were, wouldn't move out of for twenty years, through the births and growing of their daughter and son and her everlasting knitting of his shroud. After a storm seemingly sent by Poseidon tore the exposed tar paper off, the wandering family, squabbling like sailors, searched for a house. His wife rejected each one; they all failed to suit her for mostly good reasons, he recalled after she finally found a favorite, and they brought the cat home. It died, not unexpectedly, while she subjected our hero to the test of the bed. *How did it become rooted in the living room?* he wondered. At work, his colleague, the lotus eater, committed suicide; then, the one person who had praised his soothing voice suffered a brain aneurysm while making impassioned speeches to the gods. No one knew what to say. When his most immature coworker, failing to get a promotion, took an indefinite leave of absence, their boss told our champion not to procrastinate in using his cunning intelligence to do double duty. While his steadfast Penelope remained reluctant to order her household, our hero burbled to himself how to tread water; but his assistants, their ears stopped, drowned. Hearing his requiem sung by Sirens, he unlashed himself; then, as his wife's eyes rolled back in her head from his disturbing activities, he shot to the surface of the whirlpool his voyage had veered into.

The Trojan Horse

Hiding my heart inside its treacherous entrails, I—muscular, nearly naked—haul the huge hulk of reconfigured metal I bound with barbed wire away from the ravaged shell of my father's docked ship into his city, leaving it in the central square, the barren one meant for the statue of him aiming at an invisible enemy, the only kind he sees since he blindsided himself, trading the queen of his heart for one with a horn of plenty.

At the rock base of Athena's temple, I spy him—now a weak old man—weeping for his sacrifice. Bent under the weight of his charmed life of destruction, staggering to ascend the wreaked monument to the lost goddess of war and wisdom, he loses his footing and falls. From his searching wife and son, he rejects all aid. In hindsight, he was always suicidal though I only saw him trying to kill me, his sole daughter. Why didn't I discern which incidents were meant to be self-slaughter? It would take an inquisition to determine the true causes of all the near misses. Not that I wished him dead yet.

That night he creeps down the black basement stairs seeking solace from his treasure and throne. In the morning his kin curse him for endangering himself. He responds regally: "Don't you ever talk that way to me!" It is the way he talks to them. Turning, he invites me—now draped in the costly tunic he awarded me— on his walk to the city center. Recalling all those times he thrust me onto his untrained studs then stepped away, I refuse. Instead, I lead his men, the free ones, to his remaining fleet. Fearfully anticipating the moment the bearer of his fate, opened only at his command, explodes, I regret my mission and dispatch his fastest courier to bring him aboard.

Trickster Meets Whirlwind Woman

Trickster returns to his cave, the morning sun caught between his hands. Not knowing what to do with it, he places it in his man-bag with his other accoutrements—his collection of broken boundaries, his pocket calculator for creating arguments, and the book of words he carries so he can find himself when he is at a loss: vapid, innocuous euphemisms for the literati who praise his playful Celtic arrogance. In the distance he sees Whirlwind Woman watching him, a hungry ghost some say. He wants to catch her. She could be handy for filling dead air and centering himself on like a gyroscope.

He lays down his gifts along his trail: his cell phone number, his mailing address, his land line connection. "I am so turned on by you," he says. Drawn by his high frequency into his den, Whirlwind Woman sees another woman lives here. She'll have to be careful. She's known for killing wives. "No expectations, no limitations, girlfriend," Trickster warns. "I don't want to get in trouble, so don't botch this." Whirlwind Woman agrees to his contradictions. She wasn't going to settle down anyway. She never does. "What's your favorite sexual fantasy?" he inquires. "I always ask people. It reveals so much." Then his neighbor comes by with an empty wheelbarrow, and Trickster has to run.

"I had a holding dream," he tells her when they meet again. "A daydream that I was holding you. Somehow you got away without telling me what your fantasy is." She remembers swirling her tongue across the heart of his cheek, the fragile resistance she encountered on his neck, her teeth edging the tension in his shoulders massaged so tenderly by the teenaged girls in his support group for them. When she became aware of him not being there, she felt sick and held her pillow to her heart, hard, wondering if he was having her dream, too. "My fantasy is what you just told me, only I am holding you." Her lips move in. "Don't mark me," he says. But he is already marked, shining so she could see him galaxies away. "You're awesome," he offers. "I love you madly." "I love you, too," she says quietly so he can hear. As he whirls away, she stands still.

Inverting the Panopticon

Lucifer, transformer of the world, one cloven hoof raised, spins
in his goat's head at his guard tower top, instructing his crew
to complete the construction at the center of his plantation:
a panopticon. Around the tower like the mill wheel of progress
toppled, prison cells spring up, grinding their enslaved occupants
honest. Supervised at taxpayer expense, the criminals restore
churches, country clubs, and private schools for their captors then
construct prison cells for coming generations. Like mushroom
clouds in a third world war, their numbers and needs proliferate,
creating entrepreneurial euphoria.

Into this Ponzi scheme to redistribute funds cowardly collected
from falsely frightened citizens comes Gangster Game Boy who
got arrested for building a life-size, mock panopticon with his
unemployed—now incarcerated—artist friends in the abandoned
junkyard that was his city, a performance piece these street
mercenaries permanently occupied like the one they're now in.
Their performance continues with their bodies, incised with their
autobiographies in ink, encircling the central tower, tattooed
arms and legs pinwheeling in patriotic formations, watching their
watchers watch them and teaching their keepers to be creative
by refusing to be killed in this nefarious atmosphere. The monk's
life of solitary, stacked beds, silence, and semiskilled labor has
converted cell after cell into study centers for self-regulating
resistance leaders including guards who lost their jobs when
prisons were privatized, and they turned to crime in this cyclic
economy. Their homeless families camped on the perimeter await
conjugal visits in an ever-shrinking land of the free.

Under the direction of the Gangster, former inmates, now
prison guards, disseminate word of the daily art shows in the
exercise yard. Press coverage includes inmates arriving in
station wagons with out-of-state plates—traded commodities on
the gladiator entertainment market—and Lucifer being solicited
by businessmen and heads of government agencies, their black-
windowed cars identified by former-guard inmates. Under this

multicultural gaze, the rocky pit at the base of the tower shakes until Lucifer, surrounded by his captors as the tower crumbles, plea-bargains for mercy, naming the prison-industrial complex's investors. With his incarceration, the inversion of the panopticon is complete.

The Ultimate Movie Night

Selected for a study set up to see who will fall prey to the myth of the dying kingdom ruled by the king who cannot die or live, the poor, shy, young soldier plays the game, his powers multiplied by those who arm him at a small arms showcase where sophisticated shoppers buy more guns, more bombs for more battles that fund supplicants mining gold to inject into their masters' hollow hearts and stimulate their life forces.

Masked in their circuitry, the novitiate watches on the big screen his virtual self in harlequin fool's clothing kneel on medieval black and white tiles to kiss the small, gold ring he places on the wedding finger of the Virgin's statue before him. Twelve blanched nuns carrying golden candelabras lead him out the dark chapel aisle.

As, unbolted, the arched doors fan open, he sees the resurrected sun flashing on wings of angels crossing the arid land but soon distinguishes twelve knights with bewitching, burnished metalwork descending into the sands of a sacrificial valley studded with tall crosses, escaping his pursuit of them.

Distantly, hawks circle. In their shadow, a stone enclosure surrounds a castle, its drawbridge down and gatehouse broken open. On the castle's checkerboard floor, the twelve nuns offer a glowing grail of holy light to the supine, moaning king who rejects it. Turning, the nuns enter the knights' gauntlet of twelve crossed swords, coming to the uncourted naif with the seductive cup erupting like the sun from St. Peter's baptismal font. He dips his finger in, touching his forehead, his heart, and one golden drop to his tongue, the liquor of pure understanding.

The projected film reflects on the faces of those watching their trainee from the control booth as his digitized double guides the knights accompanying their debilitated king on his bier out of the disappearing castle toward the stupefying sun. In return for her directions, the kingdom's ugliest, grizzled, wizened hag asks the youth to kiss the small, gold ring she holds up to him. His fool's bells jingle as he refuses. She rides her dun mule off admonishing him.

That night at the cold campsite to comfort his ravenous
companions, the apprentice promises to kiss the next maiden
he sees. In the morning, they trek toward an immense tent.
The knights have heard its lord is so large he more than fills it.
At its doorway a desirable damsel awaits her liege's return, holding
on a silver platter the head of the last knight who passed there.
As our unworldly warrior selects her ringed finger, we are
transported back to the theater where his handlers seize him.

In the control room a grizzled, wizened dominatrix orders
twelve compellingly armed combatants to code-ready the young
scout's apartment; then, above rows of black and white tiles, she
observes the usual film fare—wars, mass shootings, and armed
murders—on computer screens monitored by delighted demiurges
while the thirteen loyal crusaders and their king reach the sea.
The animated novice pulls a long thread from the hem of his
roughly woven surplice and fishes. From a single fish, all are fed,
restored to resplendent vivacity as is the long-desiccated kingdom
behind them.

At the apartment, the twelve men tell the neophyte he is the
only knight who can bring the king to life. He must throw fresh
stones among the armies of enemies who sprang up when the king
slew their dragons and they sowed their dragons' teeth. These foes
have stolen all the kingdom's guns and warehoused them. Left un-
defended, blight has covered the land, infidels have overtaken it,
and the king and his people have withered. The innocent agrees.

They shave his head, strap on the terrible toys he will test for
them, and re-rig his metal facial disguise. On their chessboard
they illustrate the moves to make on the black- and white-tiled floor
then take him to the World's Fair of guns. As he steps two spaces
forward, one across, revolving through the globe's treasure chest
of universal ruin, the surrounding gun-hunting crowd—restricted
by the dominatrix's orders to security—is unable to run. After the
slaughter is taped, live and unrehearsed—a tool to fuel more power
shopping—the dominatrix extends her ring to be kissed by the
victor because, good knight that he is, he has financed the
restoration of her youth.

Decompositions

Blackness Behind Light

It's not just the red grapes of my poverty I eat unobserved at Walmart or the unmistakable charisma of cherries tasted up close for their blackness behind their light. It's not just that everything is connected except when it's not, the way flakes of past glimpses of you flutter down like a planeload of fool's gold exploding through the barriers of noise you make to hold yourself up to your blackness behind your light. It's just that elliptically oblique is the most hopeful way to see the world or how I hope it sees me with my rogue impeccability when occasionally my blackness hides behind my light.

Sentences Received After Sublimating Unholy Unhappiness

"You are the only one having trouble with this system. Everyone else loves it. They all say how much faster it is. Are you using the new access code? Did you enter your information correctly? No one else has complained. Don't you raise your voice at me. Why are you yelling? Yes, you are. I've never seen you behave this way. Did you follow the instructions I gave you? Now you are insulting my intelligence. I know more than you think. No, there's nothing I can do for you. I am very upset by this." Few beings have transited the third dimension without incurring negative karma. I had to apologize for two days.

Prison Planet

The Great Decider like the muses never dreamed of confronts the
chronically combustible on this prison planet by sending them pure
white light until they stop bashing dishes and clomping in the
kitchen late at night and move to a sonically more resonant place,
a form of compassion we should emulate rather than just making
out in our cells with our discontented colleagues while our minders
evaluate our performances. We bipolar pagans in anachronistic
dramas must fall face to face with the cant we invoke, mistaking
x for y in our thought problems and *zero* for *zenith,* until the gold
fingers we crave become commonplace and release us.

Portal Ends

"Hello, my dear," I say into the whore's misty, dark portal so she'll know who's visiting her wine-scented valley. A warrior who doesn't know how hard she'll have to hit or how often, she always goes where she's called. Fairies follow her; one or two feet high and not entirely benign, they plague her, flashing beams of changing colors in her eyes until a grid appears, and she must make a choice about which regulations apply: those that designate right and wrong or those elucidating paths for everyone. She can't trust the media to report these policy options. They never know why when we raise and kiss the small silver cylinder of ashes it ignites, spreading fire to light the crimes we commit against ourselves—what other crimes are there? And they never know what other policies there could be. Through their end of the portal the world looks so homogeneous, monotonous, and slight.

Always Lost

The puppet master priests, their shadows shifting on the scrim they perform behind, are burning the incandescent moon tonight as a warning to those of us looking for a messiah to arrive according to the calendar. A siren screams and screams, creating a shell of sound, while the play is performed in silence on a stage of twelve concentric circles etched with lessons from those mis-stepping their most skillful moves and slipping into the business of creating mental illness out of memories of other people's madnesses performed upon them. We are our own madnesses. We are our own messiahs. We are mendicants begging for mendacity, seeking the sacerdotal offering of a forgotten cord leading back to the love we strive for as we suffer the tyranny of misbegotten systems of slavery handed down from father to son; and Death, that arriviste, threatens to make good on his promise to steal away the secretly suicidal to unconsecrated ground where tourists pay to pray. The priests, their hair flaming, avoid the distraction of voicing directions as they lead us through the halls of our hallucinations lit by the brutal torchbearers of our previous actions. Like fire in ice we thrash, forgetting we're just making this up until the next thing happens, and we arrive at our next home.

Cover Letter

For three years I have guided tours at the Western Memorial Museum's Diorama of Enigmas where I programmed mannequins to pose as audience members prostituting for their pimp boyfriends playing Russian roulette. This exhibit is closing, and I am seeking a similar position at Infinite Gaming Technology in your Department of Marketing and Metarepresentation. My experience in disabling capacities for self-awareness via fictions about the boundaries of the human would be useful in writing, public relations, advertising, graphic design, and web development. As an expert at finding confused people huddled in corners posing as office furniture, I have proficiency at leading them astray. My taskmaster's degree in Digital Humanities has prepared me in cross-cultural manipulation of hypocrisy and computing inorganic substance abuse through self-disclosure and evidence-based cubical modifications. As a curator of novel external representations, I could contribute to your duplicitousness by creating optimal visual-spatial entertainment pretense experiments for your staff and focus groups. Because recognition of one's own cognitive processes is essential to accepting fact, I hope you will consider my attached résumé when determining the indifference behind my potential and the fluidity of my reasoning and explication to estimate the fit of my application.

Low Tensile Strength

The Valentine's rose metal soldering my corroded heart went
molten, solidified, and was bent, all in one night, then the next
morning remelted again at the soft, heated image I engineered
of you—the high-velocity, multiple-reality coach—when I said,
"I am terminally smart," and your reply reverberated in my head:
"Intelligence is the greatest aphrodisiac." It sounded so good.
I couldn't believe you could handle those words, that you were
ambidextrous in aphrodisiacs like I was. I didn't say it's my
terminal boredom that causes me to break down my usual
relations like rusting rebar cracking the concrete encasing it,
destroying whole bridges, especially kinesthetic ones, collapsing
them shortly after construction. It is beyond opulent. "You have
my attention," you said. "Do you trust me with your phone number?
Can I call you when I want to talk to you? Can we get together face-
to-face?" Your job was talent requisition while mine was industrial
mechanics: "Though it would be thrilling, I live eleven hundred
miles away. You live with someone. If you can figure something out,
let me know." You didn't say you had figured something out years
ago. "I'm married—happily married—please don't contact me any
more—sorry for being so slutty," you responded, causing me some
unexpected structural crumbling. When I saw on your profile you
had just joined *BeNaughty,* my durability in this environment failed.

Tableaux Vivants

St. Sebastian, his head in a horned helmet, rides through the woods shooting arrows at believers tied to trees. They are there to learn to forgive him. His is the harder task. The narcoleptic nun's head droops as he pierces her heart. All night she prays in her sleep; all day she sleeps during prayers, so her Mother Superior assigned her to beg for attention. Her punishment is to accept rejection. She tells herself to smile as St. Sebastian shoots her again. "Most of your audience will not be able to grasp what you are communicating," her Mother Superior has said.

On this eve of the Blessing of the Animals, the nun offers stories at supper to amuse St. Francis: of Great Rabbit who made the world of mud that Muskrat brought from the bottom of the sea and Wolf who stole the sacred sack of Death and unwittingly released it into the world. St. Sebastian and his followers demand she present a PowerPoint of pictures. When she cannot produce this, they forbid her to speak. She would like to scream, but there's no point in being histrionic, she reasons. Excusing herself, she walks down the hall to begin the long night's work she dreads. *Oh dark horse, not yet, not yet,* she counts on her rosary beads.

"I hope none of you are foolish enough to believe in a Creator," St. Sebastian, forked through with feathered arrows, announces at the morning service. St. Francis nods noncommittally as he brings forth a lone, lowly sparrow abandoned in the Garden of Gethsemane. St. Sebastian signals to begin a long hymn to insincerity. *They should really get rid of St. Sebastian,* the nun thinks but, remembering the power of thoughts, asks for forgiveness and blessings for this spiritual centurion of subtle understandings.

A young woman brings her cat to the altar. "Don't let my kitty die. Don't let my kitty die. Don't let my kitty die," she pleads. "I'll be a good girl." St. Sebastian stares skyward from his martyr's tableau, not looking at the young woman, the nun observes, realizing she will have to be the one to lead her to the grieving room.

The Tower Beyond the Wall

Love is always increasing or decreasing, she reminds herself as she takes the first step up the gritty wall she has encountered in the dark. Its length is immeasurable, but she can reach the top with her extended hand. With each step, the wall dissolves beneath her and rises above her as she reaches again. "Blessed are they who persecute themselves," the Ancient of Days said, "for they cannot escape." She realizes the wall is made of letters her disapproving sister slipped her in Bibles, now covered in elemental mud.

"One thought of light balances a thousand thoughts of darkness," she recalls. She pictures light, and the wall is gone. Before her unfolds a plain filled with women washing dead babies, baptizing them. This is what they disputed before her sister departed, her sister who thought only washing could save her. "Doesn't each soul determine its own fate?" she asked. Now the answer comes: Her fate was to accept or reject her sister's faith and negotiate the passage that ensued. Crossing the plain where each woman is her sister, each infant's name is Loss, she improvises —*I am the Fire cast upon the world; as above, so below, a twin flame blazing as the Indivisible One*—and holds thoughts of white light above her head so another wall won't block her.

Before her, four triangles converge in a pinnacle of power: the Tower of Babel where the world's people explore their voices on this ziggurat oriented towards Orion's Belt. God never said, "We shall confound them," but freed us to scatter and confound ourselves as she and her sister have done. She enters the Tower labyrinth. At its core she finds thirteen fast friends playing at the mystery, shuffling slates of knowledge lost and yet to be discovered, time having collapsed around them. "The yield will be vast though the workers are few," they tell her as the walls shift into new configurations that ring out higher, new gamelan chords. *These are my people,* she perceives, so she will wait here for her sister to arrive beyond the bang and pain of words.

Sightings

Facebook Issues

Dear Ones, as the battle for your hearts and minds heats up, make use of those famous Facebook lists and quizzes: 25 Random Relational Uncertainties, Wandering Walk-In Requests and Contacts, Multi-dimensional Karmic Clearing, Which Esoteric Extraterrestrial Are You? etc. While the Dark Forces resort to their familiar practice of trying to put you in a fearful state by diverting your attention away from the more important mission in life, remember that all the time you are living out your contract with your reality.

Activation Instructions

Guides riding the elevator politely point the way to the stars, channeling a current through your body you have not felt before. On the roof like a monumental generator, God distends in a broad band of comfort filling you with powers beyond your comprehension exactly as Tesla's mathematics show. There are pirates out there sending adverse signals—nothing stops or weakens them—but we are electrical people—biocosmic transducers—who can modulate electromagnetic fields in beneficial ways to prevent the poles from further shifting.

More Than Enough

Crop circles rain down like sacred stones from our forgotten
sky, healing Earth and all upon her through energy patterns
downloaded from cosmic medicine wheels. White, yellow, red,
black—we scramble to grab attendance as time leaps, and we ride
a new line of thought, letting go of fear, judgments, and self-doubts
—another far-left professor's liberal agenda that will be posted in
our report to the universe. Though our return date has not yet
been consciously set, our star families are waiting where we last
left them. There has been grief enough—more than enough.

Along the Milky Way

Through the breath of sacred geometry, our small neighborhood is entering an expansive phase in which light casts no shadows and amnesia is cleared away, revealing encoded secrets and multiplying our sources of inspiration. This is best understood in the fifth dimension where angels of Divine Will know each heart by name, by tone, and hold the physical dimensions in place: a complex science completely within our understanding. Lack is of the earth while love is integral, surrounding us. Circles within circles, worlds within worlds, dreams of separation dissolve as the veil thins and a new firmament rises.

Sacred Triangle

At the apex of the Community Council she was called to create out
of antiquated religious memorabilia an omniversal symbol uniting
our heart chakras to the ground that capitalism had unsanctified.
In a heap of artifacts she found a holon suited to her purpose: the
planet with its unique perceptual experience. What could separate
its cycles from its space? Surely not the prayers of missionaries on
their Roman militaristic marches wanting to be relieved of their
Adamic memories. Offering a three-pronged oration, she asked
humans to upgrade themselves as our few true prophets did
through corridors now open to all of us: to love one another as
our godlike natures yearn for; to comprehend our overarching,
inchoate free will; and to remember every moment our cellular
mother, Earth, who attracted us to spread the tale of her radiant
splendor throughout the universe.

Repeating the Experiment

They crucified Christ on this planet, and we came anyway to raise Earth with our minds and bodies barely able to function, impaired by angels who crippled us as they fell. Eons ago, a mishandling of the materials of understanding from deep within this complicated toy conceived from breathing caused an implosion with galactic implications. Dismembered, the toy reconfigured at a lower vibration, slowed and wobbled into an axial precession of twenty-six thousand years through a sub-universe located at the outermost limits of Creation reached only by half-spectrum Light. Her power lines lay broken, her path forward blocked. Cognizant of the escape gates closing, a rescue was orchestrated. We are part of it now, learning to fire thoughts in the right geomancy sequence, rebuilding complex bridges inside countless shattered cells, and anchoring the frequencies needed to rehabilitate the collapsed light/sound grid to increase our connection with Creator Consciousness.

Born Dead Under Silver Smoke Dissolving

The scenery was beautiful in this fourth world, but our thinking wasn't much after we closed the openings to the tops of our heads. Our time of useful consciousness is running out as we rush forward or backward depending on which channel you consult, forgetting that, like us, Earth grew more complex as she unfolded our twisted strings from fins to fingers, from scales to feathers, from ganglia to brains, possessing more wisdom than we can explain. Think about it next time you complain. Her skin has been closed over by our proliferating flesh, her meridians severed that run her life force, her lungs bleed ruined rivers into the sea, pierced with the metallic powder we spread in the air as we engineer the sky to hide materials more dangerous: the metallic powder that shifts the weather from the have-nots to the haves in a misadventurous imbalancing game—the metallic powder she has never had to breathe in four billion years. Already she can barely hear what we are saying. She's too weak to talk. From all around us electric blue light knocks on our sealed heads, the rescue remedy only we can administer. Faith or logic—which will win? If her soul leaves, it won't come back again.

Pick Your Past

Approximately four hundred million years ago in an adamantine rainbow of thought linking sky to earth, Source sacrificed itself, transmuting into matter, and dark angels of life too tiny to see dropped onto this planet—us. Clandestine vaccines embedded in our genes by previous interplanetary generations made us forget, but now we are remembering when we were microscopic shrimp in a tumescent sea. Though some still live where the light has not shined for twenty million years, there are none the Light has never entered into. *You do not know what it took for you to get here,* our blue jewel communicates to us, and suddenly four billion years of sacrifice makes sense—from all the cells to all the souls willing to live and die under any circumstance. We selected steersmen have left our stars to gather here at holy hours in hallowed places to raise Ascension ladders up to the stargates and bring tranquility down. Arcturian pilgrims, come to assist, welcome us to their ships' healing chambers. We go by nature into the higher frequencies, leaving behind what no longer serves us, coming back shaking our heads sympathetically at our former disorientation: Since we are emptiness, how did the dust collect?

Quickening of the Young in the Mother Womb of the Deep

Having fooled ourselves into believing the laws of cause and effect didn't apply to us, we watched our great civilization—that under the Law of One had achieved the highest harmonics on our planet—sink—lost to the fireworks we contrived but could not control. Setting forth in ships, we survivors seek the crystal caves our star ancestors charted for us, leaving inside their living stone messages on how to instruct Earth's plates to shift, resurrecting our continent.

Cumulus clouds mount on the horizon as chaos arrives faster the closer we get to our goal. Old answers do not suffice, and old systems fail. The deck is strewn with our dazed companions staggering under an incoming load of authenticity so unlike the misinformation we have been nurtured on; the ones already driven mad are locked in the hold. Our navigator, discovering the magnetic migration lines have moved causing confounded whales to beach themselves on unexpected grounds, calls Sedna to send support to the myriad sea creatures who can no longer balance the unbuffered changes in the biosphere assaulted by our barbaric behaviors and beliefs.

"You can't continue your evolution in a body that is at this level of existence," our captain says, guiding us to release our guilt and expand our understanding by conquering our contrived cultural constraints and activating our higher brain structures storing boundless history in sacred seed atoms. The Central Sun is setting on our present ship of Darkness; it will rise on shimmering new ships of Truth. If we do not see their silhouettes on the horizon with the fresh cargos they bring, it is because their configurations are not what we are expecting.

Outbreaks

Maps, Eden, and the End of the World:
A Sacrificial Festival

A cult of madness haunts the background. The images are choreographed to perform a function: Angels could fall in, or the presenters could kill the audience. Spinning golden balls of light descend, singing in rapture. Does this sound true, or would it be better to deconstruct it?

Children of the Sun

The devices issued to them now mutate their adverse reactions, and with the medicines they receive, they just run and run and run, accepting or rejecting the consciousness created for them while expanding in gratitude for everything that is. Rising up the universal tree of life on omega waves, they circumvent automatic submission to multiple false guesses by following the truth. Beneath thousands of pink slips drip-drying in schoolyards across America, disks of colored stones lead them on.

Double-Knotted

Every morning, shoelaces double-knotted, we check the clock and take off. With persistence we outperform the quadrupeds in our quest to know what love looks like. There is no predetermined path through this rugged life of alienation and mediocracy; we make it up out of what our souls tell us to seek. May you wish for yourself what you wish for others when, protected by their cars, they cut you off in the crosswalk or come at you head-on though the other lane is free. "We are not worth more. They are not worth less," S. Brian Willson said after the train filled with ammunition cut his legs off as he tried to stop its progress, suddenly seeing the radical relational mutuality that ties us all together like shoelaces double-knotted in a perpetual center place unfolding all at once.

Mass for the Dispossessed

Please pray for us despairing servants armed with candles making slow footsteps down the muddy mountain path we carried relics of eagles up. Passing weapons of mass destruction bandoliered around the shoulders of the world, we watch vendors create self-portraits in convicts' mirrors, mesmerizing us, while metaphysical scholars get rich divining the density of these sweating merchants' souls. Imagining even the sun doesn't like us, we retreat to the shadowed ruins of the temple and huddle together watching television in the dirt. Unconscious of its consequence, we concentrate on what we don't want, consuming the holy alphabet of the creators of the world then feeding it to our selfless, starved planet in a disaster of desecration. Afraid to eat fallen fruit, we compete for loaves and fishes stolen from us by those whose profits we insure by paying them double indemnity. As clocks ticking forward and backward cheat us out of peace, friends from afar beam us living energy intelligence, causing our naked hearts to burn up in the iridescent void of possibilities. Nature's laws, just and sustainable, are "like attracts like" and "the strongest force wins." When we master thought creation collectively, evil will disappear, and we will say the name of God correctly.

A Revelation of Reversals

What do knights fight for? the Knight of Mirrors tries to recall as he
gazes at his eyes muted in the reflecting glass. He knows he used to
know: In college when the Lord of Misrule, pounding his caduceus
against the floor, lived in his spare bedroom, the Knight of Mirrors
guarded him with his life until the topsy-turvy reveler died enacting
the winter solstice sacrifice, and the sorrowful knight adopted the
simpleton's disguise he has been stuck in since. *Why do knights
journey?* To bring their ephemeral selves from the long, crooked
road of reliquaries they love to pilgrimage on to an exalted city
spawned somewhere off the map by blind sages receiving prescient
messages from Stonehenge oracles. Here the subjective is more
real than the objective; the dream more real than facts; alabaster
streets shine from neither sun nor moon; and sublimely projected
structures inspire elevated thoughts. *What is the Holy Grail?
Why is it worth the hunt?* It's the cup that captured Christ's
blood of eternal life; we want to capture this cup, too, that this
priceless property be transferred: the alchemist's rule. The knight
remembers these calls and responses from when the world was flat,
four horses were coming and the wrath; but new testaments are
appearing in palimpsest texts, covenants leaping geometrically to
a quantum entanglement of truth knights are called to transmit.

The Union of Bliss and Emptiness

Before we enter the spiraling temple of distillation, the path of rose petals curving to its white center is lined with beings drawn to its light. Outside, the bride, floating on tones beyond her understanding, busily greets interchangeable strangers chanting their foreign versions of her holy name while the groom lingers in the arboretum, praying, enraptured in luxuriant isolation, as I arrive covered in stitches, their child who conjured them, wanting to give them both away.

The bell chime fades into remembered vibrations as our pensive party advances to the altar, what happened and what we imagined conflated in the caves of our brains. Surrounded by painted blue gods and goddesses ecstatically mating in the foam of samsara, we climb the stairs to the soaring *baldacchino* to see all we cannot see. Having created each other in our own images to make ourselves visible to ourselves, we die to all we think we are not and all we hope to become. Rising above delusional relationships, our most cherished disappointments drop away.

Like hollow stones, our hearts crack open, blissfully unfolding to the emptiness of union with our Creator. Releasing our desire to shackle each other and make permanent each moment of change, we shift instantly to a new energy state. Expanding God as we expand, we fulfill the purpose for which our souls were made. People are still wandering in, but we will go ahead anyway, home to where the real work begins. That is the secret to the universe.

Primal Light

Before there was anything, there was Light because endless Light is what Creation is. Spreading and slowing, the Light became the multitudinous cosmos designed on one timeless, etheric tree. Microcosm and macrocosm—all contain it, and it contains all, uniting science and spirituality. At the sovereign center of one free-will zone with great diversity, the essential tree appears to mortal eyes as two—a tree of good and evil separating above from below and day from night, conflict unreconciled—and a tree of everlasting life only gods can partake of.

Heroes travailed in the underworld to learn of the tree at its roots: Many journeys marked the seasonal changes; other sojourners sought to recover lost loves; Psyche learned to discipline her heart, saying "no" to worthy souls in her survival test; Odysseus heard his fate. When Aeneas, seeking the future of Rome, the city he was to found, plucked the tree's one golden bough for Hades' queen, another sprang forth.

Jesus, the great ouroboros uniting the two trees, arrived not to atone for sins but to teach transcendence, a lesson those who try to kill the self-renewing snake on his cross deliberately misrepresent. As he said in Hebrew, a language intoned throughout the stars, he had authority to lay down his life then to take it up, to exist in many places at one time, and to allow his body to disappear from the tomb when it was no longer important to him. He did rise and walk through walls, heal the sick and maimed. To reach the Father by way of the Son is not to submit but to emulate, not just in thoughts and deeds but in higher vibrational energy—the fruit of right thoughts and deeds and of apprehending the way back to Primal Light.

Original Sins

We never left the garden; we drove her spirit into Inner Earth. We forgot our prayers to the sun; still, it shined. We forgot to dance, but rain came. Forgetting to bless the holy water, we drank abundantly. We stopped sprinkling seeds on fallow land, yet birds sang. We forgot we came from a world where nothing grew but thoughts of God and felled trees to make statues of new gods then fought over which false image was correct. Cain, the settled farmer, slew Abel, the foraging hunter, to fertilize his crops with his brother's blood. The crops were fruitful and multiplied as the gods did when those who controlled fire made the priests pray and peasants spin themselves into gold until more who controlled fire came with guns and melted the gold in forges that fired everywhere the gold went—gold with a deep, pure light that reminded us of where we had come from more than the garden now did.

Statues gleamed, baths ran hot and cold, women wore bright jewels, and there was wine—glowing ruby red—as the garden declined. Her birds forgot to sing, rain forgot to come, and the rain that came forgot to end. When our anger grew, the garden poured her molten core out, reflecting our anger back. When our tribes opposed each other, the garden trembled then split, horst and graben, in frustrated imitation of our rifts, until those who understood her responses called on their guides in the worlds without gardens. Five thousand came on a lava beam that replenished the garden's hollowed-out core. Others healed with tools that those who had become Death, Destroyers of Worlds, weren't allowed to have. Still more came singing on quivering wings. The garden's multitudinous saviors polished her halo with their thoughts of love. She breathed again, her life energy restored, and from Inner Earth her spirit rose.

Psyche in the Noosphere

Wandering ceaselessly away from my companions' trail of common
choices leading to love talk about who deposited or deducted what
the day the house payment is due or long office after-hours,
earbuds tuned to *YouTube,* avoiding a small monster in after-school
daycare--I have become lost at the peak of an inescapable mountain
where referencing myself I find nothing. After I regard my death for
seven days--tasks unfinished, words unsaid, opportunities not
pursued--the great, carrion-eating condor parts the clouds with
lightning from his eyes, exposing the lesson in each event.

Seeking the inhuman bridegroom within my inhuman self,
I ride this thunderbird of prehistory into the cracks of the earth,
past unsorted, scattered seeds of potential lovers who wanted to
adore me for being the fertile, cleared ground they could write
themselves upon—or right themselves upon—after marrying
unfurled wildflowers that blossomed into hues that jarred them.
Dropping deeper into the *shhhh* of the wind, I observe the golden
rams I wished to play among and their killing strength from the
head-butting they thrive on; then, I spot Pandora's box broken
open on the trail leading from the caves of Lascaux where
humanity first imagined its Source and made art.

Flying along the cascading stream of life, I scoop and sip.
We lift up. Along the walls exactingly extracted scorpion devils
of unconsciousness crawl. Buffalo-horned sentinels stand in the
slits consuming this internalized negativity. On the earth's plain,
twin samurai, swords unsheathed, skirts of skulls dangling from
their waists, crouch ready to sever the headful of limitations
I must separate myself from to enter the spectrums expanding
far beyond my receptivity. Here angels and devas dwell, and we
hold hands in a ring rising through thought fields filled with
catastrophic event horizons whose outcomes we redirect with
our collective intent, raising the sphere of awareness until all
phenomena disappear into particles traveling faster than light.

Acknowledgments

Grateful acknowledgment is made to the following publications in which these works first appeared.

Front Range: "Burying the Dead Horse"
Opium Magazine: "Pueblo Dog"
Earth's Daughters: "Desert Passages"
200 New Mexico Poems: "Gallery Talk"
The Rag: "Our River Guardians"
Howl: "The Bardo of Our Idolatry," "Super-Slip Boundary Conditions"
Flash in the Attic Flash Fiction Anthology: "Relinquishing
    Underwater Parallax Delirium"
pacificREVIEW: "Mass for the Dispossessed"

"Burying the Dead Horse," "Pueblo Dog," "Churchyard Statuary," "In an Off-Season Sublet Where Beeswax and Ambergris Burn," "Far Harbor," "Desert Passages," "Gallery Talk," "Facebook Issues," "Activation Instructions," "Along the Milky Way," "Maps, Eden, and the End of the World: A Sacrificial Festival," and "Children of the Sun" appear in the chapbook *In a Cosmic Egg* (Finishing Line Press, 2012).

The quotation from S. Brian Willson in "Double-Knotted" appears at www.brianwillson.com.

*Cover art, "Frenzy," by Lee Passarella (lpassarella.artspan.com);
cover and book design by Diane Kistner (dkistner@futurecycle.org);
DejaVu Serif text with Arial Black titling*

About FutureCycle Press

FutureCycle Press is dedicated to publishing lasting English-language poetry and flash fiction books, chapbooks, and anthologies in both print-on-demand and ebook formats. Founded in 2007 by long-time independent editor/publishers and partners Diane Kistner and Robert S. King, the press incorporated as a nonprofit in 2012. A number of our editors are distinguished poets and writers in their own right, and we have been actively involved in the small press movement going back to the early seventies.

The FutureCycle Poetry Book Prize and honorarium is awarded annually for the best full-length volume of poetry we publish in a calendar year. Introduced in 2013, our Good Works projects are devoted to issues of universal significance, with all proceeds donated to a related worthy cause. Our Selected Poems series highlights contemporary poets with a substantial body of work to their credit. Our flash fiction line presents quick reads that can be serious or light-hearted, irreverent or quirky, fantastic or futuristic, or just plain fun.

We are dedicated to giving all of the authors we publish the care their work deserves, making our catalog of titles the most diverse and distinguished it can be, and paying forward any earnings to fund more great books.

We've learned a few things about independent publishing over the years. We've also evolved a unique, resilient publishing model that allows us to focus mainly on vetting and preserving for posterity the most books of exceptional quality without becoming overwhelmed with bookkeeping and mailing, fundraising activities, or taxing editorial and production "bubbles." To find out more about what we are doing, come see us at www.futurecycle.org.

www.ingramcontent.com/pod-product-compliance
Lightning Source LLC
Chambersburg PA
CBHW070943250626
47159CB00009B/3364